No Naptime for Janie!

No Naptime for Janie!
A Hanukkah Tale

written by **Margie Blumberg** • illustrated by **Renée Andriani**

MB PUBLISHING

For dearest Jane ~

Your sparkling laughter, warm friendship, and generous spirit
are what I'll always treasure . . . and remember.

For my wonderful mom and nana, who made baking — and noshing — fun!

And for Jimmeleh, my hero.

Bundles of love,
Margie

For Vince. Because sometimes, nothing but pie will do.

~Renée

First published in the United States by MB Publishing, LLC
www.mbpublishing.com

Library of Congress Control Number: 2017905037

Blumberg, Margie
No Naptime for Janie: A Hanukkah Tale/by Margie Blumberg;
illustrations by Renée Andriani

Summary: Rhyming text in English, Hebrew, and Yiddish is
accompanied by charming illustrations to present a busy
afternoon of pie-baking before the first night of Hanukkah for
Nana and her granddaughter Janie—and Sheepy, the dog.

ISBN: 978-0-9908430-6-1

Directions for peeling and coring an apple were adapted from this
RealSimple.com video: https://www.realsimple.com/food-recipes/
cooking-tips-techniques/preparation/how-core-apple

The recipe for the apple pie filling was adapted from Karen E.
Barkie's apple pie recipe in *Sweet and Sugarfree* (St. Martin's
Griffin, 1982). The topping for the apple pie was inspired by
Goldene Blumberg, the author's mother, who always added
yummy apricot jam to her delicious dessert made with apples
and sweet potatoes.

~ More Titles From MB Publishing ~
The Scoop on Good Grammar • *Breezy Bunnies* • *Sunny Bunnies*
• *Paris Hop!* • *Rome Romp!* • *Avram's Gift* • *A Gefilte Fishy Tale*
• *Tutti's Promise* • *Jake McGreevy Novels: Celtic Run* and *Chicago
Bound* • *The Secret at Haney Field: A Baseball Mystery* • *Escape in Time*

Future Titles
Busy Bunnies • *Snowy Bunnies* • *Bunny Romero's White House
Adventure* • *Paris Plunder: A Jake McGreevy Novel*

About the Author and the Illustrator

MARGIE BLUMBERG writes and publishes books for all ages, from toddlers to adults. Her own books are *Avram's Gift, Paris Hop!* and *Rome Romp!* (Books 1 and 2 in the Travel Adventures with Grandma Goldie series), *The Scoop on Good Grammar*, and the Carrot Cake Park Tales series, which so far features two picture books—*Breezy Bunnies* and *Sunny Bunnies*. Ms. Blumberg is also the publisher of *A Gefilte Fishy Tale*, written by Allison and Wayne Marks and illustrated by Renée Andriani; the Jake McGreevy middle-grade novel series by Sean Vogel, with two titles in print to date: *Celtic Run* and *Chicago Bound*; R. M. Clark's *The Secret at Haney Field: A Baseball Mystery*; Ronit Lowenstein-Malz's *Escape in Time*; and K. Heidi Fishman's *Tutti's Promise*. Visit mbpublishing.com to learn more.

RENÉE ANDRIANI grew up in Connecticut and has a BFA in Illustration from the Rhode Island School of Design. She works in an array of media, including pen and ink, pencil, dye, watercolor, and digital. Her illustrations appear in numerous children's books, as well as in magazines and on Hallmark's Shoebox greeting cards. She also serves as a graphic recorder and graphic facilitator, collaborating with organizations and their teams to create visual stories that reflect meetings, brainstorms, and published content. Clients include Hallmark, HarperCollins, Dutton Children's Books, Puffin Books, Simon & Schuster Children's Publishing, Golden Books, MB Publishing, Scholastic, Penguin Young Readers Group, and Little, Brown & Company. Renée Andriani's book titles include *Paris Hop!, Rome Romp!, A Gefilte Fishy Tale, Company's Coming: A Passover Lift-the-Flap Book, Baby on the Way*, and *This School Year Will Be the Best!* An avid hiker and cookie baker, she draws inspiration from doodling in her sketchbook, being outdoors, and hanging out with funny people. She lives in Kansas with her husband, three children, and two dogs. Visit http://randriani.carbonmade.com/ to see more of her outstanding work.

balabusta or balebosteh (Yiddish) ~ a female head of household who is devoted to maintaining a beautiful home (AE: bah•luh•**buhs**•tuh [*u* in *buhs* = *u* in *put*]; Y: bah•leh•**boss**•teh; the male form is **balebos** [bah•leh•**boss**]; *o* in *boss* = *o* in *more*)

balagan (Yiddish, Modern Hebrew) ~ a mess (bah•lah•**gahn**)

bubbeleh (Yiddish) ~ a term of endearment: darling, dear, honey (**bub**•eh•leh; *u* in *bub* = *oo* in *moon*)

chag sameach (Hebrew) ~ happy holiday (khahg sah•**may**•ahkh; *kh* = *ch* in Scottish *loch*)

dreidel (Yiddish) ~ a four-sided toy that is spun like a top in a game of chance; each side is marked with a Hebrew letter (**dray**•dl; rhymes with *ladle*)

-eleh or -leh (Yiddish) ~ a suffix added to a name as a sign of affection. For example, "Jimmy" becomes "Jimmeleh" and "Marge" becomes "Margeleh" (**jim**•eh•leh, **marge**•eh•leh)

gey shlofn (Yiddish) ~ go to sleep (gay **shlof**'n; *o* in *shlof* = *o* in *more*)

gelt (Yiddish) ~ money (gelt; use a hard *g*, as in *go*)
Hanukkah gelt refers to coins that were traditionally given to children during the festival of Hanukkah. Nowadays, the "coins" are foil-wrapped chocolates.

Hanukkah or Chanukah (Hebrew) ~ literally, "dedication."
This jubilant holiday, also called the Festival of Lights,
commemorates the rededication of the Second Temple in Jerusalem
following the victory of the Maccabees over the Syrians in 165 B.C.E.
(AE: **hah**•nuh•kuh or **khah**•nuh•kuh; H: khah•nu•**kah**;
Y: **khah**•nu•keh; *u* in *nu* = *oo* in *moon*; *kh* = *ch* in Scottish *loch*)

kinder-vinkl (Yiddish) ~ children's
corner (**kihn**•dehr-**vink**•l)

kvelling (Yiddish) ~ bursting with
pride (**kvehl**•ing)

latke (Yiddish) ~ a potato pancake
that is traditionally served at Hanukkah,
often with applesauce on the side
(AE: **laht**•kuh; Y: **laht**•keh,
singular; **laht**•kehz, plural)

oy vey (Yiddish) ~ an exclamation of dismay,
grief, or exasperation (oy vey; *oy* rhymes
with *toy*; *vey* rhymes with *hey*)

shaina maidel (Yiddish) ~ pretty girl
(**shay**•neh **may**•dl; *maidel* rhymes with *ladle*)

ziskeit (Yiddish) ~ sweetness; also, an
endearing term for a child (**ziss**•kite)

Note: AE = American English, H = Hebrew, and Y = Yiddish

"It's time for a nap —
Kiss-kiss, little *dreidel*.
Tonight's the first candle.
Sweet dreams, *shaina maidel*."

"Our Janie and resting —
Like oil and water.
She'll spin like a top,
Then drop — that's my daughter!"

"I'm not drowsy at all.
How on earth can I sleep?
I don't want to lie down —
I don't want to count sheep."

"I'm up!"

"Yes, I see . . ."

"And there's nothing to do.
I suppose I'll just sit
While you knit something blue."

"I'm thrilled you're awake!
We can bake a surprise —
A Hanukkah treat
For your tummy and eyes."

"Will I really like it, Nana?"

"If you still adore apples,
I'm certain you must,
And cinnamon — yummy! —
A warm, crumbly crust,
Then surely you'll love it
Let's give it a try
For mine is the
Scrumpdillyishiest pie!"

"Flour, water,
Oil, too —
Hold the bowl and
Mix it through."

"Press it out and
Pinch, pinch, pinch.
Scalloped borders . . ."

"They're a cinch!"

"Whoops!"

"Wash the apples . . ."

"Peel the skin,
Slice them —"

"Not too thick or thin."

"Nice and easy —
Sprinkle spice,
Stir in raisins,
Shake it twice."

"Spread the filling
In the shell.
When it's done, we'll . . ."

"Hear the bell!"

DING! DING!

DING! DING!

DING!

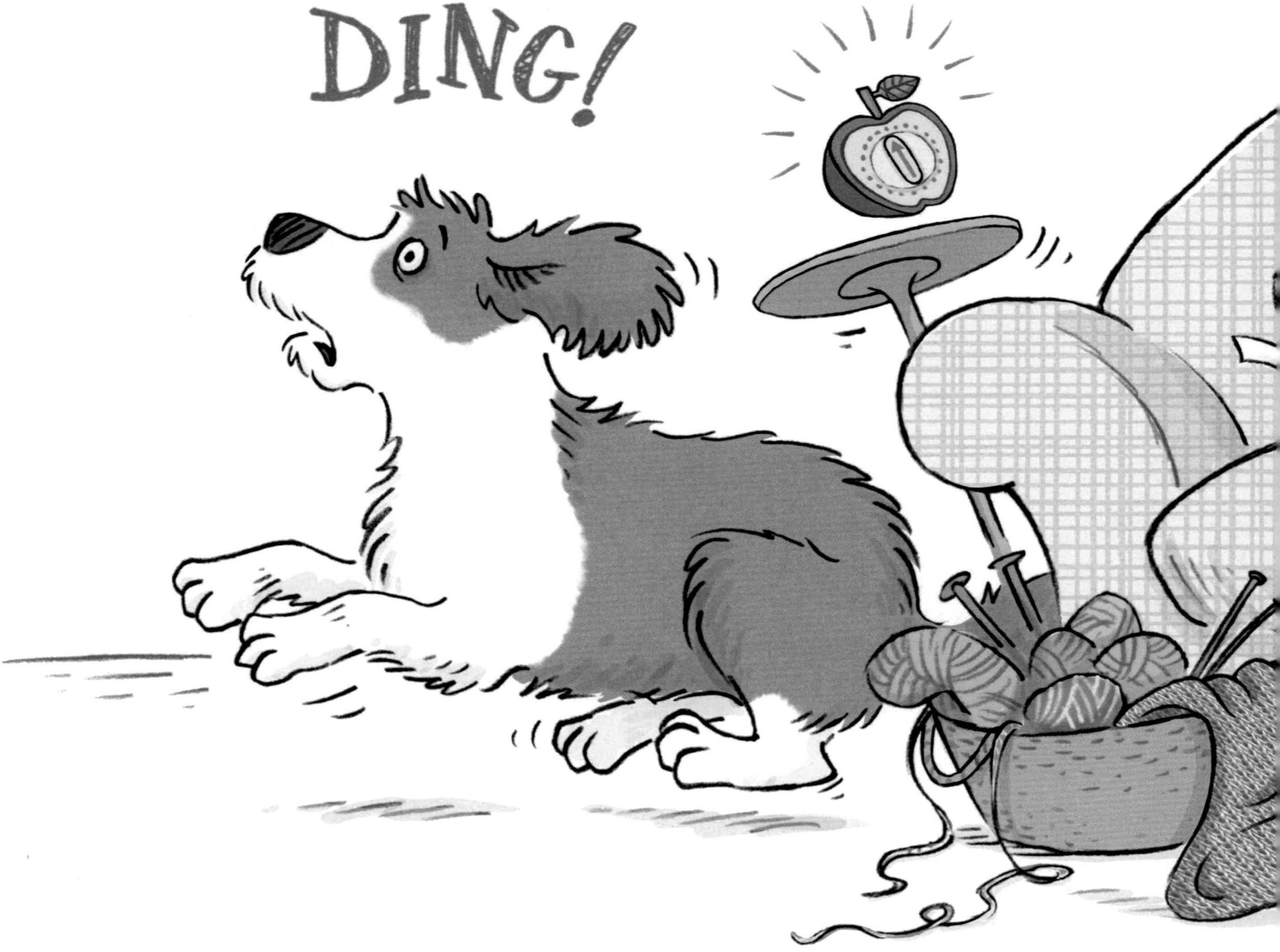

"Oy vey, ziskeit,
I forgot.
We need jam —
Sweet apricot!"

"Cans of salmon,
Bags of chips,
Yellow twists and
Purple clips."

"Peaches, berries,
Melon, cheese,
Rice and carrots,
Squash and peas!"

"Tasty rolls with almond butter —
Sifter, spoons, a cookie cutter."

"Where's that jam?
I'm getting hot.
It must be someplace
We are not!"

"Red tomatoes, honey cake —
Jamless pie's a huge mistake."

"Napkins, plates, and forks —
We're set."

"Janie,
You're too much, my pet!"

"A *balagan* —
It's quite a sight.
We have to clean . . ."

"'Cause that's polite."

"We'll . . .
Pack the cabinets."

"Scrub the tile."

"Stack the dishes
Single file."

"Squirt and scour —
Mom won't guess
That we ever
Made a mess!"

"Know what, Nana?
Now I'm sleepy.
Naptime, *shlof*time . . .
Let's go, Sheepy."

"Again?"

"Jimmeleh, Jimmeleh,
My, oh, my —
Nana and Janie
Made a . . ."

"Hanukkah, Hanukkah,
We love you.
Latkes, dreidels —
Lots to do!
Make a pie and
Sing a song . . .
Hanukkah, Hanukkah
Eight days long!"

DING-DONG!

"Chag sameach!"

Welcome to our *kinder-vinkl*. Here in the children's corner, you'll learn how to play the dreidel game, sing two new songs, bake an apple pie, and light a hanukkiyah.

Let's Play Dreidel!

You'll need . . .

- Two or more people to play
- One dreidel (or one dreidel for each player)
- *Gelt* (several coins for each player)

The object of the game is to win all the *gelt*.

1. **Look at your dreidel.**

   Each side of a dreidel is labeled with a Hebrew letter: **N**un (נ), **G**imel (ג), **H**ey (ה), or **Sh**in (ש). These letters represent words: *Nes* (miracle) *Gadol* (great) *Hayah* (happened) *Sham* (there). (Pronounce these words this way: NEHS ga•DOHL hah•YAH SHAHM.) Together they mean this: "A great miracle happened there." In Israel, the fourth side has the letter **P**ey (פ), for *Poh* (here): "A great miracle happened *here*." In the game, these letters have different meanings. See number 4.

2. **Get comfortable.**

   Sit on the floor or in chairs around a table. Deal an equal number of chocolate *gelt* coins or real coins (e.g., nickels) to each player (8–15 coins each).

3. Choose a player to go first.

Either chose someone at random, or let players spin the dreidel to see who gets the "highest" letter: the highest is Nun, followed by Gimel, Hey, and Shin (or Pey). Play continues in a clockwise direction.

4. Ante up and begin the game.

Each player places one coin in the center pot. The first player spins the dreidel once and then follows the rule for whatever letter the dreidel lands on:

- Nun (נ) stands for "nothing," so the player takes nothing from the pot. It's the next player's turn to spin.

- Gimel (ג) stands for "get," so the player takes all the *gelt* in the pot. Since the pot is now empty, all the players put in another coin.

- Hey (ה) stands for "half," so the player takes half the *gelt* in the pot. If the number of coins in the pot is uneven, divide the number by 2 and round up to the next whole number. For example: 9 coins divided by 2 = 4.5 coins, so the player takes 5 coins.

- Shin (ש) stands for "share," so the player adds either one coin to the pot or three coins (three coins for each of the three stems of the Shin). It's your choice!

5. Continue playing.

- Players need to ante up each time someone spins or whenever there are no more coins left in the pot.

- When a player runs out of *gelt*, he or she is eliminated from the game. However, to keep that player in the game longer, other players may share some coins.

- The game is over when one player has won *all* the coins in the game.

Timed variation: Set a timer for an agreed-on period. Whoever has the most coins when the timer goes off is the winner.

"Little Top, Stop Spinning"

A Hanukkah Lullaby • Words and Music by Margie Blumberg

Lit - tle top, stop spin -ning, Time to rest your head. Bliss-ful tales are wait-ing in your dreams, so off to bed. Ha -nu-kkah fills hearts with joy,* we'll play a -gain to-mor-row. But for now stop your spin -ning, the stars are be -gin-ning to twink -le and wink -le up a - bove. Gey shlof' -n, my sweet bun -dle of love.

*Use these lyrics for the rest of the year:
"Tuck this happy day away."

To listen to these songs, please visit: http://www.mbpublishing.com

"Spinning Tops and Gelt Galore"

Words by Margie Blumberg • Music from "Ma'oz Tzur"

♩ = 120

Spin - ning tops and gelt ga - lore, Dec - or - ate o - ur fes - tive floor.

Ap - ple pie with jam that's hot, Lat - kes too real - ly hit the spot. Ev - 'ry-one, re -

mem - ber Oil that last - ed eight da - ys long. Let's sing out this hap - py song,

All to - geth - er from the start. Joy - ful - ly we

play our part, Ded - i - cat - ed from the heart.

Let's Make an Apple Pie

INGREDIENTS

1 pie crust for an 8" or 9" pie plate

¾ cup raisins

¾ cup water

5 cups apple slices (approximately 5 peeled, cored, and sliced sweet-tasting apples, such as Fuji)

1 tablespoon fresh lemon juice

1 teaspoon cinnamon

Apricot jam or fruit spread (for the topping)

INSTRUCTIONS

- PREPARE your favorite crust for apple pie.
- PREHEAT the oven to 350°F.
- ADD the raisins to the water and bring to a boil in an uncovered saucepan.
- REMOVE from the heat, cover, and allow the raisins to soften for 10 minutes. Set the timer.
- PEEL, CORE, AND THINLY SLICE* the apples and place them in a large bowl.
- WHEN THE TIMER GOES OFF, pour the water and the raisins into a strainer over a small bowl.
- SPOON in and distribute the raisins among the apple slices.
- DRIZZLE AND DISTRIBUTE the lemon juice throughout the apple-raisin mixture.
- SPRINKLE in the cinnamon, a little bit at a time, tossing the apples and the raisins as you go to ensure that they are coated evenly.

- TRANSFER the filling into your unbaked pie shell.
- BAKE for 40 minutes or until the apples are tender.
- COOL on a wire rack for 60 minutes. Serve.
- TOPPING INSTRUCTIONS: Before serving, place a desired amount of apricot jam (depending on the number of servings of pie, this amount will vary from a few teaspoons to ¼ cup or more) into a glass measuring cup or a glass serving bowl. Warm it in the microwave on the lowest defrost mode. Remove after a few seconds and stir. If not warm enough, heat again for a few more seconds. Stir again. Repeat if necessary. If too hot, allow the jam to cool a bit before serving on individual plates of pie or in a serving bowl.
- REFRIGERATE the pie for up to three days. If you are not serving the pie immediately, cover with foil and refrigerate.

* To begin, on your cutting board, cut off the top and the bottom of an apple to create two flat bases. With a Y-shaped peeler, peel the skin at the top and the bottom only, each in one circular motion. Use the same peeler to peel the rest of the skin. Peeling top to bottom, remove the skin in strips. **Slicing instructions:** Stand the apple upright on its flat base and cut the apple with a sharp knife, close to the core. Set this first piece aside. **Second slice:** Rotate the apple so that it is flat side down and cut the apple close to the core. Set this second piece aside. **Third slice:** Rotate the apple so that it is again flat side down to make your third cut (close to the core). Set this third piece aside. **Fourth slice:** Finally, rotate the apple one more time, flat side down, to cut the last piece away from the core. Discard the core. Cut the four apple pieces into slices.

Let's Light the Candles

Candles are added to the hanukkiyah* (the nine-branched candelabrum, or Hanukkah menorah, pronounced hah•noo•kee•**yah**) from right to left, but they are *lit* from left to right. In other words, each night, the candle placed last is lit first. (The Hanukkah candles are lit before the Shabbat candles on Friday night and after Havdalah on Saturday night.) Here are the step-by-step instructions:

1. On the first night of Hanukkah, place two candles on the hanukkiyah. As you face the hanukkiyah, one candle is set in the candleholder on the far right. The other—the *shamash* (the helper candle, pronounced **shah**•mehs in Yiddish and shah•**mahsh** in Hebrew)—is placed in the candleholder that is either higher or lower than the other eight.

2. Light the *shamash* with a match. Remove this lighted candle from its holder and use it to light the other candle. Only the *shamash* is lit with a match.

3. On the second night, place *three* candles on the hanukkiyah: the *shamash* and two candles next to each other, beginning on the far right. With the lighted *shamash*, light the other two candles—again, left to right.

4. On nights three through eight, repeat this process, adding one new candle each night. On the eighth night, your hanukkiyah will look like the illustration!

*Also spelled **chanukkiyah** (pronounced khah•noo•kee•**yah**; *kh* = *ch* in Scottish *loch*).

4881782BR00033

Made in the USA
Middletown, DE
28 September 2017